A Visit to a Car Show

Jill McDougall

Illustrations by Dale Newman

Last weekend,
Grandpa took me to a car show.

Grandpa knew that I had always wanted
to visit a car show.

I was so excited!
My favourite racing-car driver, Erik Jansen,
was going to be at the show.

CAR
SHOW
ENTRY

As soon as we arrived,
Grandpa and I went to look
at the really old cars.

My favourite car was a Model T Ford.
It had big round headlights
and a soft roof that could go up and down.

Grandpa said that this Model T Ford was much older than he was! It was built in the 1920s.

After that, Grandpa took me to see the hot rods. He knew I would like them, and he was right!

The hot rods were cars that had been fixed up to go fast and look cool.

Most of the hot rods
were painted in bright colours.

One old purple hot rod had the bonnet taken off.
Grandpa and I had a good look
at the huge engine.

Then, we went to look at a big hot rod with flames painted on the side.

Suddenly, the owner turned on the motor and ... **vr-oo-m**! The big car shook and the engine roared like thunder.

This made everyone cheer.

After we left the hot rods,
Grandpa and I went to look at a few electric cars.

These cars don't use petrol to run.
Their power comes from electricity.
It is stored in a battery inside the car.

The owner of the electric car
took us for a ride.
We only went for a short distance,
but it was exciting.

The motor was really quiet.
The only sound I could hear
was the noise of the wheels on the grass.

After lunch, Grandpa and I went to the racetrack to watch the racing cars zoom by.

One by one, the drivers sped along the track. They wanted to show how fast their cars could go.

Suddenly, I saw Erik Jansen in his shiny red car! He was waiting for his turn to race along the track.

His engine let out a roar and off he went.

Erik's car was the fastest of them all!

Later, the racing-car drivers
parked their cars by the track.

People were able to get a close look
at all the racing cars.

Then, I saw Erik Jansen standing by his car!

I felt shy but I went over to him
to say hello.

Erik Jansen was very kind.
He let me sit inside his car!

I held the steering wheel,
and I felt as if I was in a race!

Grandpa took a photo of me with Erik Jansen.

I was so happy that I couldn't stop smiling.

A short time later,
Grandpa and I left the car show.

It was a great day!

I can't wait to go to another car show with Grandpa.